W9-CBH-311

DISNEY's
Aladdin
ABU AND THE EVIL GENIE

by Michael Teitelbaum

Illustrations by Yakovetic

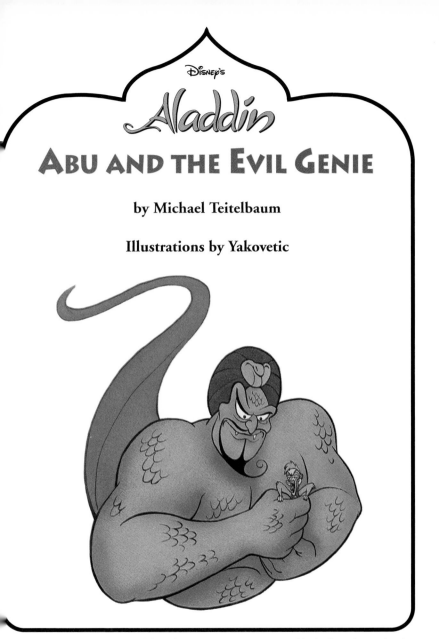

©1993 The Walt Disney Company. No portion of this book may be reproduced without written consent of The Walt Disney Company. Produced by Mega-Books of New York, Inc. Design and Art Direction by Michaelis/Carpelis Design Assoc., Inc. Printed in the United States of America.

ISBN 1-56326-253-3

CHAPTER 1

top! Thief!" shouted Daoud, the fruit merchant.

Aladdin and his pet monkey, Abu, dashed through the streets of Agrabah. Aladdin was tossing apricots to Abu, who put them into a sack.

"Hurry, Abu!" shouted Aladdin, clutching the apricots.

Daoud, who was waving a sword, grabbed Aladdin by the arm.

"Got you, thief!" the merchant bellowed. He swung the razor-sharp sword.

Aladdin ducked and pulled free. "This way, Abu!" he shouted. "Quick!"

Abu squealed and followed Aladdin down a

dark, narrow alley.

More merchants carrying swords joined the chase.

Aladdin pitched the last apricot toward Abu, and stopped short: The alley was a dead end! They were trapped, and the merchants were closing in.

Swords glinted in the morning sun. Aladdin looked around. Abu was nowhere in sight.

"Abu!" shouted Aladdin. "Oh, no! Abu is gone!"

"You've stolen your last apricot, thief," cried Daoud. He raised his sword….

Aladdin jumped up in a panic. He looked around the bedroom and realized he had just had a nightmare.

Aladdin relaxed and stretched when he saw that Abu was snoring in a nest of pillows at the foot of his bed. "Oh, Abu," he said, "I'm so glad you're safe. I dreamed we were still poor, stealing apricots in the market. Then you disappeared."

Abu patted Aladdin's head and yawned.

Aladdin was sitting up in his feather bed,

with silk sheets and a handwoven blanket. Elegant carpets hung on the walls.

But he and Abu had once been beggars on the streets of Agrabah. The only bed they had then was a straw mat; the only food, what they could beg or steal.

All that changed for Aladdin when he found a magic lamp containing a genie who granted him three wishes. Aladdin freed the Genie of the Lamp with his third wish. Instead of his master, Aladdin became the Genie's friend. Aladdin was now a prince, and he and Abu lived in the Sultan's palace.

One thing had not changed: Abu was always hungry. He pointed to the rising sun and rubbed his stomach.

Aladdin laughed — the nightmare was over. He got out of bed. "Let's have some breakfast, Abu," he suggested.

Aladdin and Abu were soon seated at a low table. Aladdin peeled a banana and took a big bite, but Abu was struggling to get the stopper out of a bottle of apricot nectar.

Abu pulled and pulled. Finally, straining with all his might, he yanked the stopper out.

Thick green smoke erupted from the bottle and filled the bedroom with a smell like rotten eggs.

Abu dropped the bottle and ran up Aladdin's arm onto his shoulder. Aladdin coughed. His eyes were tearing. "What on Earth was in that bottle?" he asked.

The green smoke swirled around Aladdin and Abu. Then it began to take on the shape of a man.

Finally, an enormous green genie stood before them. He was staring straight at Abu.

CHAPTER 2

 am Ashab Khan!" The genie raised himself to his full height. His turban, fastened with a clasp in the shape of a snake's head, brushed the ceiling. His green skin was scaly, and toes like claws stuck out of his leather sandals.

"Oh," said Aladdin. "It's another genie. Looks like you've got one of your own, Abu."

"You are wrong, young prince!" bellowed Ashab Khan. "I serve no master."

"What are you talking about?" replied Aladdin. "Genies always serve those who release them. Abu is now your master."

Ashab Khan laughed. "You speak the words of the good genies I have known," he said, "like the one who created that magic bottle and trapped me inside years ago."

"Then you're not a genie?" asked Aladdin.

"Oh, I am a genie all right. I am Ashab Khan, the All-Powerful — and slave to no man!" he roared.

Ashab Khan stared at Abu. "You, monkey, freed me from the bottle. Thanks to you, I can return to my home. And you are coming with me — as my slave!"

Ashab Khan grabbed Abu and flew out the window, leaving a trail of foul green smoke.

"Abu!" shouted Aladdin. He rushed to the window. "Bring him back, you over-grown lizard!" His shouts echoed through the palace.

Princess Jasmine had just finished dressing when she heard Aladdin shouting.

"What has that monkey done now?" she wondered. She ran down the hall to Aladdin's room to find out.

Aladdin was leaning out the window, still calling Abu.

"What's wrong?" asked Jasmine.

Aladdin told her about Ashab Khan.

"Well, what are we waiting for?" cried Jasmine. "We have to go after them."

She raced to the corner of the room, where Aladdin's Magic Carpet was rolled up, still fast asleep.

"Can you believe it?" asked Jasmine, pointing at the Carpet. "It could sleep through anything!"

"Wake up!" shouted Aladdin. He unrolled the Carpet.

The Magic Carpet rubbed itself with its tassels to wipe away the sleepiness.

"We need your help!" cried Aladdin. "Look!" He pointed to the window. "An evil genie took Abu."

The Carpet glided to the window and looked out. Spying the poison-green smoke, it zipped back to the corner, curled up, and cowered in fright.

"Come on, Carpet," Aladdin said. "If you don't help us, we'll lose his trail!"

Reluctantly, the Carpet unrolled and hovered above the floor.

"Hop on!" Aladdin said to Jasmine.

They leapt aboard the Carpet. "Follow that smoke," cried Aladdin. "And hurry, Carpet! Hurry!"

The Magic Carpet zoomed out the bedroom window.

CHAPTER 3

 railing green smoke, Ashab Khan raced high above the city of Agrabah and was soon over the desert.

Abu bit Ashab Khan's hand, then spat out a mouthful of horrible, jagged green scales and shuddered.

"Ha! Ha!" laughed Ashab Khan. "You don't find my skin tasty? Feel free to take another mouthful, you little monkey. They grow back. Look!"

He held up his hand. New jagged green scales had replaced the ones Abu had bitten just a moment before.

Abu kicked and punched Ashab Khan's

arm. "Stop tickling me," said Ashab Khan.

Abu sighed and gave up. He watched the ground rush by beneath them.

"It is no use, little monkey," said Ashab Khan. "You are my slave, and nothing can change that!"

Ashab Khan was flying toward a canyon. It looked as if someone had torn a huge gash in the desert floor. A deep, wide opening in the sand ran for miles in either direction.

"We are almost home," said Ashab Khan. "Once we get there, no one will ever find you."

Abu began to struggle again. Ashab Khan laughed at the monkey's useless efforts. Then he focused his attention on their journey. Abu squirmed out of his vest and dropped it after they crossed the canyon.

"Oh, poor pitiful creature," said Ashab Khan. "You lost your vest. Well, don't fret. We'll find something else for you to wear when we get home. Something not so easy to lose. Ha-ha."

Abu moaned and stopped struggling.

The Magic Carpet picked up speed. Aladdin and Jasmine gripped its edges as it flew faster and faster.

"I can't see them!" Jasmine shouted.

"Just follow the green smoke, Carpet," said Aladdin. "We're lucky it's so thick that it hangs in the air a long time."

"I don't know of a village or an oasis in this part of the desert. Where could that crazy genie be taking Abu?" asked Jasmine. "And if he's all-powerful, how can we ever get Abu back?"

"We'll get him back," Aladdin vowed. "Nobody can steal my buddy and get away with it."

The Carpet sped above the golden sands. "The smoke is getting thinner!" cried Jasmine. "We're losing the trail!"

"Faster, Carpet, faster!" cried Aladdin. But by the time the Carpet reached the canyon, the green smoke had disappeared.

The Carpet slowed and hovered over

the deep canyon.

"What now?" asked Aladdin.

Suddenly, the Magic Carpet bucked and pointed its tassels across the canyon.

"Are you sure?" Jasmine asked.

The Carpet flew to the other side and pointed down with a tassel.

"Look!" Aladdin shouted, pointing to the sand. "It's Abu's vest! They must have come this way. Good work, Carpet. Let's go." The Carpet flew straight ahead.

At last Ashab Khan slowed down.

"We are almost home, little monkey," he said.

They flew over the desert a while longer. "Ah," Ashab Khan sighed. "Home at last."

He stopped in midair and waved his arm. The air shimmered, then rippled like a silver curtain blowing in a gentle breeze. The shimmering curtain opened and the sweet smell of fragrant flowers filled the air.

"Welcome to your new home, slave." With a cackle, Ashab Khan flew through the opening. Just before the curtain closed, Abu tossed his cap backward. Nothing remained on the other side except the endless desert sands. And a tiny cap.

CHAPTER 4

he Magic Carpet smashed into a wall. Aladdin and Jasmine tumbled to the sand, stunned. The Carpet looked like an accordion.

Aladdin looked up. All he could see was sand in all directions.

He got to his feet. "Are you all right, Jasmine?"

"I'm fine — just confused. What in the world did we hit?" She stood up. The Carpet unpleated itself and rested in the sand.

Aladdin stepped forward and bumped his nose. He reached out with his hand and felt a smooth, solid surface.

"There's something here — it's like an

invisible wall!" Aladdin said.

"Look!" Jasmine said. She bent down and picked up Abu's hat.

"This wall must be Ashab Khan's work," said Aladdin. "I'll bet he and Abu are on the other side."

"How do we get in?"

"We can't go through it," said Aladdin, slapping the wall. It was hard as granite. "Maybe we can go around it. If we travel sideways we may come to the end of it."

"What are we waiting for?" asked Jasmine. She dropped Abu's hat in the sand to mark their place.

Then they climbed aboard the Magic Carpet and flew along the wall.

Every few minutes, Aladdin reached out with his hand to touch the surface. "This could go on for miles and miles," he said.

At last they saw Abu's hat in the sand. They had followed the invisible wall in a complete circle.

"We can't go through it," said Jasmine, "and we can't go around it."

"What if we went over it?" asked Aladdin. "It can't go up forever. It's worth a try." He patted the Carpet. "Head for the sky, Carpet!"

The Carpet flew straight up. Soon the air grew cold and thin.

Aladdin's turban flew off. "I'm freezing," he said. "Guess the turban wasn't going to keep me any warmer." He could see his breath in the chilly air.

"We've got to go higher," said Jasmine. She hugged herself for warmth.

The Carpet kept ascending. Every now and then it reached out with its front tassels to feel for the wall.

"We can't go much higher," said Aladdin. "We'll pass out."

The Carpet shot straight up to where the air ended.

"Hold your breath," said Aladdin.

Jasmine began to grow dizzy.

The Carpet reached out. Nothing!

It raced over the wall and down the other side. Aladdin let out his breath.

"You did it, Carpet! You got us over

the invisible wall."

Jasmine took a deep breath. "Nice work, Carpet," she said. "Let's go where it's warm."

Moments later they were hovering on the other side of the wall.

"It's an oasis," said Aladdin.

"It's so green in here!" said Jasmine. "It's like a park — no, a garden."

Palm trees and flowers swayed in the warm breeze. Streams flowed in all directions. Fountains splashed everywhere. And in the distance, a waterfall poured over the edge of a cliff.

"This must be the home Ashab Khan mentioned when he took Abu," said Aladdin. "They've got to be around here somewhere."

Aladdin, Jasmine, and the Magic Carpet flew deeper into the oasis in search of Abu.

At the center of the oasis, near a rushing stream, Ashab Khan snapped a shackle onto Abu's ankle. A thick metal chain led from the shackle to a heavy ball that glowed with a sickly green color.

"You see, slave?" said Ashab Khan. "I told you I'd find you something to wear when we got home. Ha-ha!"

Abu sat down and moaned.

"That will keep you from running away," said Ashab Khan. "Now, bring me some figs from that tree over there. Then fetch me a jug of water from the stream."

Dragging the heavy ball and chain behind him, Abu struggled to the tree and plucked some figs. Then he trudged to the stream, plunged the jug into the cool water, and filled it. He could barely lift it.

The Magic Carpet burst from behind a flowering bush.

"Put that down, Abu!" shouted Aladdin. "You don't have to serve him. You're coming back with us!"

Abu tossed the figs into the stream and dropped the jug. He tried to run to Aladdin, but the ball and chain held him back.

"Well, well," said Ashab Khan. "A rescue team has arrived. Now the real fun can begin." Ashab Khan pointed a finger at the sky.

Two giant vultures appeared and dived down toward the Carpet. Aladdin and Jasmine leapt off and landed on the grass. The birds flew up and away.

"Are you all right?" asked Jasmine.

Aladdin's eyes opened wide. Slithering toward them was a sea of snakes.

"Watch out, Jasmine!" yelled Aladdin. "They're poisonous!"

The deadly snakes advanced on Aladdin and Jasmine, who turned to run. More snakes were closing in from every direction.

CHAPTER 5

laddin grabbed the Magic Carpet and held two corners in each hand.

"Sorry about this, Carpet," he said. "I don't know what else to do." Moving fast, he scooped the snakes into the Carpet.

The Carpet took it from there, skimming along the ground, scooping up all the rest. It spun at top speed, then let go of the snakes, sending them flying to the farthest corners of the oasis.

When it landed, the Carpet shook itself from top to bottom.

"Very clever, boy," snarled Ashab Khan, "but I tire of these games." He glared at Abu.

"Slave! Gather twice as many figs and twice as much water. Now!"

"No, Abu!" said Aladdin.

Abu shrugged and slowly walked toward the fig tree.

"As for the two of you...BE GONE!" cried Ashab Khan. With a wave of his hand, he sent Aladdin and Jasmine flying away. They passed through the invisible wall like rain through an open window and sailed out over the desert.

"Carpet, where are you? Can you hear me?" shouted Aladdin.

"Ashab Khan must have kept it!" said Jasmine.

"Then I think we're in trouble!" yelled Aladdin.

He looked down as they sailed through the air. Too quickly, the desert came up to meet them.

"We're going to crash!" Aladdin cried. Then he saw it: an enormous catcher's mitt waiting for them. Jasmine and Aladdin plopped down into the mitt.

"Yooou'rrre SAFE!" They heard a familiar

voice call out.

"Genie! Am I glad to see you!" said Aladdin.

"No kidding, Al," said the big blue Genie, who gently set Aladdin and Jasmine down in the sand. "People are always saying that. Especially people who are plunging to their doom."

"How did you know we were in trouble?" asked Aladdin.

"When Ashab Khan escaped from the bottle, it was all over the genie grapevine," the Genie said. "So I hightailed it to Agrabah. I've been following your trail since you set out on this little joy ride."

"Genie, do you know Ashab Khan?" asked Jasmine.

"Everyone knows Ashab Khan. He's what we genies call one baaaad dude!"

"I didn't know there were any genies who refused to obey masters," said Jasmine.

"Well, we have seventy-two different genie tribes, with seventy-two thousand in each tribe. Each one rules over a thousand Marids, each Marid over a thousand Afrits, etcetera, etcetera, etcetera. There's bound to be a bad apple now and then," said the Genie with a shake of his head. "Ashab Khan's not really big on obeying a master himself. He's more into control. Making a slave obey him means more to Ashab Khan than anything else."

"But how did he end up in that bottle?" asked Aladdin.

"Long ago," began the Genie, "Ashab Khan had an argument with another genie over some apricot orchards that belonged to that genie's master — a nice farmer over in Syria. After a struggle, the farmer's genie tricked Ashab Khan into drinking a bottle of apricot nectar from a magic bottle the farmer's genie created for the occasion. The bottle sucked Ashab Khan inside and the genie plugged it up so tight no human could open it."

Aladdin laughed. "That fits," he told the Genie. "It wasn't a human who opened it. It was Abu. He forced it open, and out came Ashab Khan."

"It's terrible, Genie," said Jasmine. "Now Ashab Khan's got Abu in chains, forcing him to carry figs and water."

"Sounds like old Ashab, all right," said the Genie. "He always had a weakness for fruit. Come on, guys, hop on board. It's time to squeeze this lemon once and for all."

Aladdin and Jasmine jumped into the Genie's outstretched arms.

"Genie Shuttle *Big Blue* on the launch pad. 10-9-8-7-6-5-4-3-2-1-blastoff!" shouted the Genie. He rocketed into the sky and flew off toward the oasis.

"Ahh, the old invisible wall trick," said the Genie when they had landed a few seconds later.

"I don't see anything," said Aladdin. "I didn't see it last time either." He rubbed his nose.

"You're not supposed to," said the Genie. "Being a genie myself, I can always spot a barrier made from genie magic."

"I hope we're not going to fly over the top of the wall again!" said Jasmine.

"Nah. Too easy," said the Genie. "Old genie proverb says: 'Where there's a wall, there's a way.'"

The Genie snapped his fingers and a giant blue key appeared in his hand. "Stand back, genie at work," he said. He shoved the key against the invisible wall.

Blue and green sparks flew when the Genie turned the magic key in an invisible lock.

"I can smell the flowers from Ashab's oasis," said Aladdin. "You've opened it."

They stepped into the lush paradise. The Genie tossed the key onto the grass near the invisible open door.

"Hey, nice place he's got here," said the Genie, looking around. "I wonder who his decorator is."

They made their way to the center of the oasis. Soon they were face-to-face with Ashab Khan, the All-Powerful.

Abu dropped the jugs he was carrying. The Magic Carpet flew out from behind a tree to Aladdin's side and wrapped a tassel around his hand.

"So! You have returned," snarled Ashab Khan, "and you brought a good genie back with you."

"Hey, there, Old Greedy," said the Genie. "Still into the slave thing? That's my friend you're forcing to haul your water. You *want* water? You *got* water."

The Genie snapped his fingers and an oversized jug appeared above Ashab Khan's head. The stopper popped out and the jug turned itself over, spilling water all over the wicked genie.

Abu laughed, and the Carpet clapped its tassels.

"For my next trick," continued the Genie, "I free the little guy."

A blue bolt of the Genie's magic headed straight for Abu's shackle. But before it arrived, Ashab Khan fired off a green bolt, blocking the Genie's shot.

"You have invaded my paradise!" bellowed Ashab Khan. "You know the consequences of such an intrusion, do you not, Blue One?"

"I do," said the Genie. His face looked

grave. "If you insist, I challenge you to *Dosh-Ka* — a full-scale battle of genie powers. If I win, my friend Abu goes free!"

Ashab Khan smiled an evil smile. *"Dosh-Ka* it shall be. I accept the challenge."

CHAPTER 6

shab Khan waved his arms.
Aladdin looked around in surprise. They had been transported out of the oasis to the middle of the desert. Jasmine and the Magic Carpet were next to him, and the Genie stood a few feet away. But Abu was still trapped inside the oasis.

Not far from the Genie, Ashab Khan sat cross-legged on the sand.

Aladdin walked over to the Genie. "What's going on?" he asked. "What's this *Dosh-Ka?*"

"*Dosh-Ka* is the most serious challenge one genie can issue to another," the Genie said. "Even our nasty friend there has respect for its tradition and power."

"Do you fear *Dosh-Ka*, Blue One?" shouted Ashab Khan. "Why do you hide behind your mortal friends?"

"Clear the decks, sailors. Batten down the hatches," said the Genie. "This is war!"

Aladdin, Jasmine, and the Carpet moved away.

"I fear nothing, Evil One," the Genie called back in the same serious tone Aladdin had heard him use earlier. "I respect the time-honored traditions of *Dosh-Ka*. Let us begin at once." The Genie sat down and took up the same cross-legged position as Ashab Khan.

Both genies began to chant words Jasmine and Aladdin couldn't understand.

Then the chanting stopped.

"DOSH-KA!" screamed both genies at the same time.

"Since you issued the challenge, Blue One, the law of *Dosh-Ka* says I cast the first spell," said Ashab Khan.

He waved his arms. The ground began to rumble, and hundreds of mounds rose up from the sand. The mounds took on human shape. Within moments, an army of soldiers made of sand had formed.

Line after line of sand soldiers marched in step across the desert, in the direction of Agrabah. The dry ground shook with each step they took.

"Pretty fancy stuff, Mr. Green-genie. Sorry to spoil your parade, but —"

The Genie snapped his fingers. A whirlwind swept across the desert. The mighty winds blasted the rows of sand soldiers apart, scattering sand into the sky. Once the sand army had returned to dunes, the whirlwind slowed to a stop.

"Amazing!" said Aladdin.

"Which part, the sand soldiers or the whirlwind?" asked Jasmine.

"Both," said Aladdin.

"My turn," said the Genie. He snapped his fingers. An elephant emerged from the funnel of the whirlwind, which then disappeared. The elephant was fifty feet high, with a trunk that was twenty feet long.

The elephant reached out with its trunk, picked up Ashab Khan, and placed him on its back.

"I thought you'd like to go for a little ride," said the Genie. "Feel free to take it out for a test drive."

Aladdin and Jasmine laughed. "He looks like a mouse on that elephant," said Aladdin.

"You dare to humiliate me!" screeched Ashab Khan. "I'll show you a mouse!"

Ashab Khan clenched his fist. Flashing green light surrounded the elephant. It began to shrink.

When the spell was complete, Ashab Khan stood over a mouse, laughing. The mouse squeaked and ran off.

Ashab Khan wasted no time in casting the next spell. "Primal elements arise!" he shouted. "Rain fire from the skies!"

Sparks fell from the sky, like raindrops made of fire. The sparks grew into flames. A wall of fire ten feet high spread across the desert.

"A gift for you and your meddling

friends," said Ashab Khan.

The wall of fire moved swiftly toward the Genie.

"Get behind me," he shouted. Aladdin and Jasmine raced and hid behind him. The Magic Carpet began furiously digging a hole in the sand.

The Genie snapped his fingers. He was dressed like a firefighter, complete with helmet, rubber boots, and a thick hose that extended across the desert as far as the eye could see. "I've hooked it up to the Red Sea," he explained.

A mighty blast of water gushed from the hose. The Genie sprayed the water left and right along the wall of fire, dousing the flames.

"Remember," he said to Ashab Khan, "only you can prevent desert fires."

"Genie!" said Aladdin. "Nice move!"

The Genie snapped his fingers again and the sand around Ashab Khan was changed into an enormous roll of white linen. Before Ashab Khan could move, it wrapped itself around his sandals and all the way up to the turban on his head. He looked like a mummy. Then a glass dome dropped over Ashab Khan.

"Hey, look at that," said the Genie. "Mean Genie Under Glass!"

Aladdin and Jasmine giggled.

"Game over," said the Genie. "I win. Let's get Abu."

Suddenly, a humming filled the desert. It grew louder and louder, and became a whine.

Aladdin and Jasmine put their hands over their ears. "What's that noise?" cried Jasmine.

"Look!" shouted Aladdin.

"Uh-oh," said the Genie.

Ashab Khan was spinning under the glass dome like a top, creating the high-pitched whine. As he spun, the linen wrapping peeled off.

The piercing tone shattered the dome. Shards of glass flew into the sky and vanished. Ashab Khan was free.

"You boast too soon, Blue One," said Ashab Khan. "I am through toying with you.

I will show you how powerful I am. For my
next spell I turn to your precious city of
Agrabah. When I have finished, Agrabah will
no longer exist!"

CHAPTER 7

 shab Khan flew off in a cloud of green smoke, leaving a trail that led straight to Agrabah.

The Genie whisked Jasmine, Aladdin, and the Magic Carpet away toward the city.

"What about Abu?" asked Aladdin. "He must still be inside the oasis."

"No time to lose. This is an emergency," said the Genie. "We've got a city to save!"

They followed Ashab Khan's trail and caught up with him on the outskirts of Agrabah.

When Ashab Khan saw them, he laughed wickedly.

"This will be the final spell of the *Dosh-Ka*, Blue One. Now we will see who is the more powerful."

Ashab Khan clenched his fists again. Then he tilted his head back and chanted. "City of Agrabah, your end is near! I fill your streets with doom and fear!"

The ground rumbled and split open beneath the city.

High above Agrabah, Aladdin and Jasmine sat on the Magic Carpet and gazed down.

"The city is falling apart. Genie? Genie!" Aladdin shouted. The Carpet flew to the desert floor and landed near the Genie, who had not answered. His eyes were glazed over with a green film, as if he were in a trance. He stared at Ashab Khan but did not move.

"Uh, Genie…This is no time to fool around," said Aladdin.

"The Genie's in trouble," said Jasmine.

"What do we do?" Aladdin asked. "Ashab Khan must be focusing all that rage he stored up in the bottle on the Genie. He caught the Genie by surprise. It's probably more than

he can handle."

"Do something!" cried Jasmine.

Aladdin thought for a moment. Then he said, "I have an idea. Get going, Carpet."

"Where are we going?" asked Jasmine.

"Back to Ashab Khan's oasis. He's too busy with his spell to notice we're gone," said Aladdin. The Carpet took off in the direction of the oasis.

As they flew through the air, Aladdin looked back. Agrabah was covered by a green fog. He couldn't see what was happening.

The Magic Carpet sped back to the oasis. When they reached the invisible wall, the Carpet flew through the opening the Genie had made with his magic key.

Just inside the wall, Aladdin jumped off the Carpet and searched the grass.

"What are you looking for?" asked Jasmine. She stepped off the Carpet, too.

"The Genie's key," answered Aladdin. "He dropped it near the entrance after he opened the invisible door."

"Found it!" shouted Jasmine as she

picked up the key.

"Great!" said Aladdin. "Let's get Abu."

They flew to the center of the oasis, where Abu was still chained to the heavy ball next to the fig tree. The chain, like the ball, glowed green.

"Hey, Abu!" shouted Aladdin. Abu chattered with glee.

"We're happy to see you too, Abu," said Aladdin. "Are you okay?"

Abu shook his head and pointed to the chain.

"That's why we're here, pal," replied Aladdin. He turned to Jasmine.

"The Genie's key is charged with his good magic," said Aladdin. "If you use the head of the key like an axe, it might cut through the shackle on Abu's leg."

Jasmine nodded. She raised the key above her head and slammed it down on the glowing green shackle with all her might.

Blue and green sparks flew. When the air cleared, the shackle was gone! Abu was free.

He hopped into the air, then hugged

Aladdin and Jasmine.

"No time to celebrate," said Aladdin. "We've got to get back to Agrabah!"

Aladdin hurried over to where Ashab Khan had stood when the Genie first confronted him. He picked up the water jug and stopper that the Genie had used to douse Ashab. Then they all ran to the Carpet.

"Let's go!" said Aladdin.

The Carpet zipped through the air and passed out of the oasis and back over the desert to Agrabah.

In the distance, they saw a green cloud hovering high in the air.

"What's that in the sky?" cried Jasmine. "And where's Agrabah?"

"That *is* Agrabah!" shouted Aladdin in horror.

Ashab Khan had lifted the city off its foundations. It hung in the sky, high above the sand, suspended by the green glow of the wicked genie's spell. Aladdin started concocting a plan that he explained to Jasmine and Abu while the Carpet whisked them closer to the floating city.

The Carpet stopped above where Ashab Khan stood on the desert floor. Magic crackled all around him like green electricity.

Their big blue genie was still as a statue, frozen and powerless, his eyes glowing green.

Aladdin looked up at his beloved city, hanging like a precious jewel in the sky. Will my plan work? he wondered.

CHAPTER 8

he Magic Carpet dropped down until it was floating next to Ashab Khan. The power of his evil magic made Aladdin dizzy, but he took a deep breath.

"Hey, Khan! Someone's here to see you!" he called.

Ashab Khan ignored him.

"He must have to focus all his energy to keep the city aloft and the Genie in a trance," said Aladdin. He turned to Abu. "Okay, Abu, up here on my shoulder."

Abu scrambled up and stood on Aladdin's shoulder. Abu howled and screeched at Ashab Khan.

The wicked one turned his head in their direction and spotted Abu.

Rage filled his eyes. His face twisted. He charged toward Aladdin and Abu.

"What is the meaning of this? Come back to me at once, slave!" Ashab Khan ordered. Green sparks flew around him.

Aladdin grabbed the water jug he'd brought from the oasis and removed the stopper. Then he handed the jug and the stopper to Abu.

Ashab Khan reached for Abu. "You are mine," he said.

"Now, Abu!" shouted Aladdin.

Abu leaped onto Ashab Khan's scaly shoulder. He pressed the jug against one of Ashab Khan's ears. He put the stopper on the other ear, squeezing Ashab Khan's head in between.

Green and blue sparks flew as the blue magic from the jug reacted with Ashab Khan's green magic.

With a whoosh, Ashab Khan turned into thick, green smoke. The jug sucked the smoke inside. Abu slammed the stopper into the top

of the jug and sealed it tightly.

The battle was over. Ashab Khan was trapped inside the jug.

The Genie snapped out of his trance and the green faded from his eyes. "Way to go, Laddie!" he exclaimed.

"Genie, look!" Jasmine cried, pointing up.

The force of Ashab Khan's magic had been holding the city up in the sky. Now that the evil genie was bottled up in the water jug, Agrabah was plunging back toward the desert floor.

In a flash, the Genie's big blue body stretched and changed, forming itself into an enormous silk cushion. He braced for the impact.

The city of Agrabah landed on the cushion with a soft thud.

"Oy! That'll give you such a pain!" groaned the Genie. He gently slid from under the city walls and the city settled into place on the desert floor.

Then he snapped his fingers. Tipped-over carts righted themselves and broken glass became whole as the Genie's magic set things straight throughout the city. A short while later, Agrabah was hustling and bustling at its usual frantic pace as though nothing had happened.

With the day almost over, the Genie decided to fly with Aladdin and the others to the royal palace. "Nothing like a full-scale battle to work up an appetite," he said.

"That reminds me, all I had to eat this morning was a banana," said Aladdin. "I'm hungry."

"How did you know that water jug trick would work?" asked the Genie when they were relaxing in the garden.

"I remembered what you said about Ashab Khan's greed," said Aladdin. "That he couldn't bear the thought of losing a slave. I figured that when he saw Abu, he would try to get him back."

Abu danced around like a boxer and punched the air.

"Once we had his attention," Aladdin

went on, "I was pretty sure we could trap him in the jug because it was made from good genie magic, just like the nectar bottle that started this whole adventure."

"Pretty clever," said Jasmine. "By the way, what do we do with that jug now that Ashab Khan's inside?"

"I'll drop it off at the bottom of the Red Sea after dinner," said the Genie. "We'll never have to worry about Big, Green, and Greedy again."

Abu pointed at the door. The palace staff was bringing out food. Al Khayat, the royal tailor, was bringing out a brand new hat and vest, just like Abu's old ones.

"This calls for a special celebration drink," said Aladdin.

"And am I thirsty!" said the Genie. "I could drink a well full of water all by myself. What's on the menu, Chief?"

"Apricot nectar," suggested Aladdin.

Abu shrieked and dashed away, his vest only half on. Aladdin grabbed him.

"Just kidding, Abu," said Aladdin. He

turned to the others. "Pomegranate juice all around!" he ordered.

"This calls for a patented Genie group hug," said the Genie. "Hurry, let's capture the moment."

He embraced Aladdin and Jasmine. The Carpet squeezed in. And Abu climbed to the Genie's shoulder so he could join in, too.

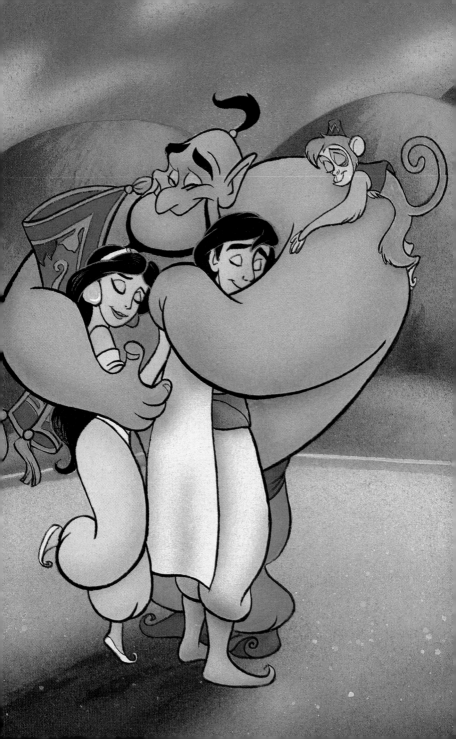